On Wimbledon Common, under the ground in their Burrow, live

The WOMBLES

Deep Space Wombles

Adapted by Elisabeth Beresford

from the Wombles television series produced by CINAR and UFTP

Hodder
Children's
Books

a division of Hodder Headline plc

Wellington was working on one of his ideas -
a Womble spacecraft.

"It's nearly perfect, even if I do
say so myself," he muttered.

He didn't see Bungo and Tomsk
watching him. They wanted to know
what was going on. . .

But before they could ask him, Wellington trotted off to the Burrow to get a special tool.

"Now's our chance to have a look," said Bungo. "Isn't it amazing!"

"Wow, it's. . . it's. . . what is it Bungo?" asked Tomsk. "Let's look inside."

"What's this for?" said Tomsk, as he pressed a button.

At once Wellington's face appeared on the Wellicom screen. "Bungo, what are you doing in my spacecraft?" said Wellington.

Bungo and Tomsk thought that calling it a 'spacecraft' was very funny. They were laughing so much that Bungo pushed against a red button without noticing.

The next moment a siren started wailing
and there was a whirring noise as the
spacecraft rocked from side to side.

"You idiots!" shouted Wellington.
"You've started the spacecraft."

And as he spoke the spacecraft zoomed
into the air with Bungo and Tomsk on board.

Wellington raced out of the Burrow
just in time to see his spacecraft flying over.
It worked!

On it went, passing over Shansi and Stepney
who were making a scarecrow Womble for Shansi's garden.
But all they noticed was the shadow of the spacecraft as it
zoomed overhead.

Bungo and Tomsk were tumbling
about inside the spacecraft.
"Wellington - stop this thing!" shouted Bungo.
"I CAN'T!" Wellington shouted back on the Wellicom.

"Where are we going to land?"
Bungo asked in a trembling voice.
  "Well, er, I'm sorry,
I really don't know," said Wellington.
    "WELLINGTON! DO SOMETHING!"
Bungo and Tomsk shouted together.
    But it was too late. The spacecraft
was floating down on a parachute.
It touched ground . . . somewhere!

Bungo whispered, "I think we've landed."
"Oh, good!" said Wellington on the Wellicom.
"What does it look like outside?"
Bungo and Tomsk stared out through
the portholes . . .

"It's not a bit like Wimbledon Common," said Tomsk.
    "Yippee, you're the first Wombles in outer Space.
You must get out and explore," said Wellington.
    "We will be able to get home again, won't we?"
asked Bungo.

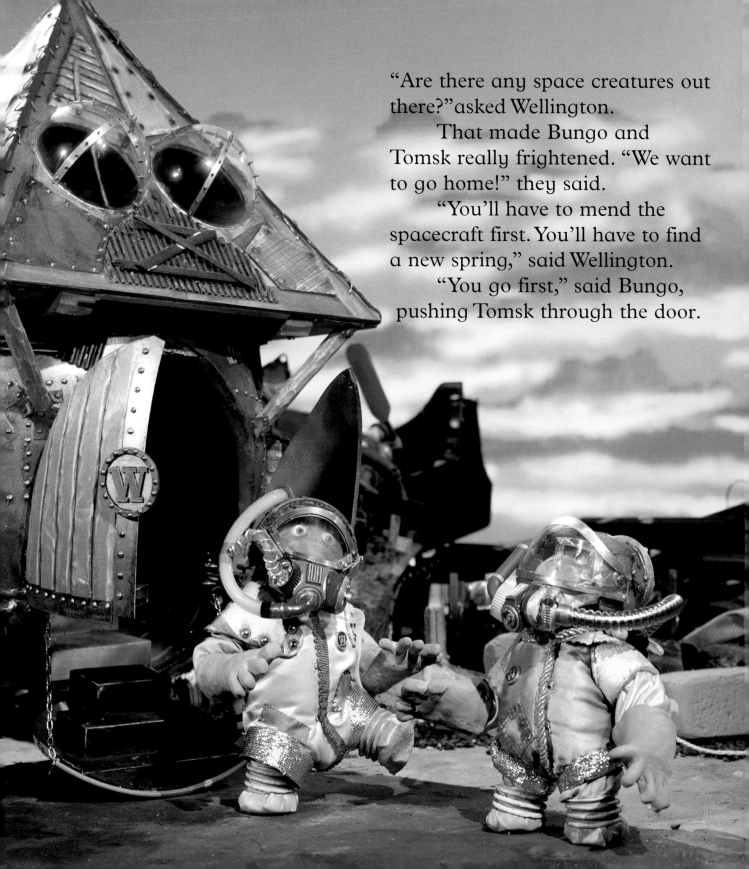

"Are there any space creatures out there?" asked Wellington.

That made Bungo and Tomsk really frightened. "We want to go home!" they said.

"You'll have to mend the spacecraft first. You'll have to find a new spring," said Wellington.

"You go first," said Bungo, pushing Tomsk through the door.

The two small Wombles got more and more frightened as they hunted round for a spring. They felt as if scary things were watching them. Suddenly Bungo slipped. Down he fell and hit a piece of wood.

TWANG! Something flew up in front of him.

Tomsk and Bungo ran for their lives. The two Wombles fell into the spacecraft and rushed to the Wellicom.

"We found a THING!" shouted Bungo. "Get us home!"

"What does the Thing look like?" asked Wellington.

"Like that!" said Bungo as it got closer to the spacecraft.

And then they saw STEPNEY, pushing his barrow with a Jack-in-the-box on the front of it! They ran out to meet him.

"What are you doing out in Space?" asked Bungo.

"I've been exploring the rubbish dump at the end of the Common. And I've just found a smashing scarecrow for Shansi's garden," said Stepney. "What was that about Space, then?"

Bungo and Tomsk looked at the Jack-in-the-box and then at each other. "Oh, nothing!" said Bungo. "Come on, it's time we went home for tea!"

On the Wellicom, a voice called, "What's happening?"

Nobody answered. They'd all gone back to the Burrow!

First published 1999

Photographs and original artwork,
courtesy of FilmFair Ltd.
a subsidiary of CINAR Films Inc.

ISBN 0 340 74671 8

10 9 8 7 6 5 4 3 2 1

A catalogue record for this book
is available from the British Library.
The right of Elisabeth Beresford to be identified as the
author of this work has been asserted by her.

Printed in Hong Kong

Hodder Children's Books
a division of Hodder Headline plc
338 Euston Road, London NW1 3BH